Dear Kinsey, Merry Christmas! Love you, Gramme + Papa

P.O. Box 448, Tonasket, WA 98855
Tel: 888-252-0411  Fax: 425-458-4319
info@howellcanyonpress.com — www.howellcanyonpress.com

*Library of Congress Cataloging-in-Publication Data*

Howell, Trisha, 1962-
   The princess and the pekinese/ written by Trisha A. Howell; illustrated by Paul Lopez
      p. cm.
   Summary: A snobby princess makes an astonishing discovery that helps her to better
appreciate her blessings.
   ISBN  1-931210-03-9
   [1. Dog—Fiction. 2. Appreciation—Fiction.] I. Lopez Paul, 1963-, ill. II. Title.
PZ7.M19867 On 2002
[E]—dc21                                                                200203477

**DEDICATED**
To Princess Lillian (1983-2001)
Little Addison (1986-)
and to every dog who has enriched our lives over the millennia.

**ACKNOWLEDGEMENTS**

Many thanks to John Thompson of Illumination Arts. Without his creativity,
knowledge and tireless support, this book would not be possible.
I am grateful as well to my mother, Frances Thomas Fike, who was very helpful
with her extensive editing suggestions. My deepest thanks also to my beloved
husband Dean, whose amazing love, support and healing energy
have filled my life with happiness.

Published in the United States of America
Printed in Singapore by Star Standard Industries
Book Designer: Peri Poloni, Knockout Design, www.knockoutbooks.com

We are a member of Publishers in Partnership — replanting our nation's forests.

# The Princess and the Pekinese

Story by **Trisha Adelena Howell**

Illustrations by **Paul Lopez**

$\mathcal{T}$here once was a beautiful princess born into a happy, loving family. Surrounded by people who adored her, Princess Lillian grew up with every privilege. She was served the finest foods and went with her family on scenic hikes through the country-side. Every day she was cuddled, and her hair was carefully brushed. Each night she dreamed of glorious adventures as she slept on satin sheets.

$\mathcal{L}$ife was perfect for the Princess—until the dog arrived. She could not imagine why her family had acquired such an animal. They already had several cats that stayed outside where they belonged and kept the house free from rodents.

$\mathcal{T}$he intruder,
a playful Pekinese puppy,
bounced endlessly through the house,
shattering Princess Lillian's peaceful life. This
unruly creature slept in a bed right next to hers and
even enjoyed the same gourmet meals!

$\mathcal{S}$he bristled whenever the dog was cuddled before she was or its hair was brushed before hers. Even though the Princess received just as much attention as before, she no longer felt special.

Princess Lillian did everything possible to rid herself of the stupid, slobbering mutt. She kicked it to interrupt its peaceful slumber. She stole its food when her parents weren't looking. She even created little "accidents" on the oriental rugs that were blamed on the new arrival. But no matter what she did, the puppy seemed to adore her even more.

$\mathcal{O}$ne morning, as the Pekinese was once again attempting to kiss her, Princess Lillian prayed for an escape.

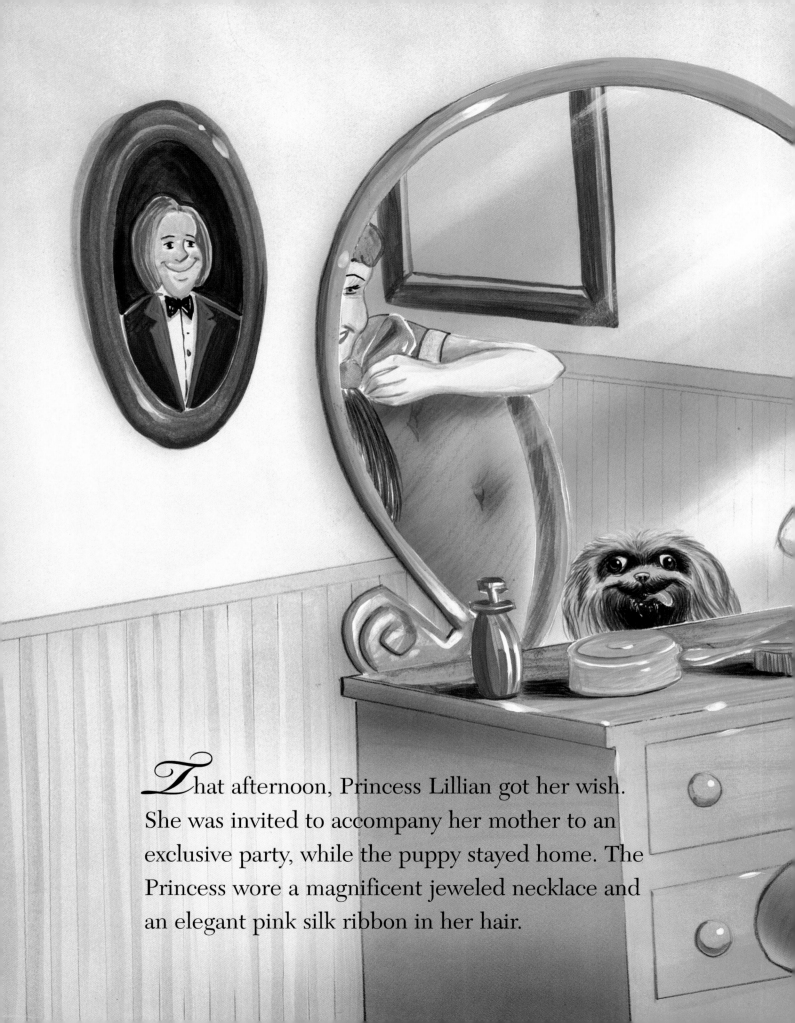

That afternoon, Princess Lillian got her wish. She was invited to accompany her mother to an exclusive party, while the puppy stayed home. The Princess wore a magnificent jeweled necklace and an elegant pink silk ribbon in her hair.

$\mathcal{P}$rincess Lillian was thoroughly enjoying the party when a lady pointed in her direction, exclaiming, "What an adorable dog!" The Princess looked all around, but there was no dog in sight, not even the dreadful Pekinese.

Another guest looked directly at her and cooed, "Such a darling little Yorkie." The Princess was puzzled.

"May I pet your precious doggy?" the hostess asked, her hand caressing Lillian's head. As she finally realized the ugly truth, the Princess recoiled in shock. It was a nightmare from which she would never recover: She, Princess Lillian, was a dog!

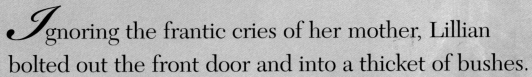

*I*gnoring the frantic cries of her mother, Lillian bolted out the front door and into a thicket of bushes.

Emerging onto the city street, Lilian ran wildly for hours. Finally, exhausted, her little legs collapsed as she stumbled into a trashy gutter. She was staring with disdain at the piles of garbage when a whack resounded in her ears. A sharp pain stung her ribs, and a drunken voice slurred, "Get out of my way, you stupid dog!"

Shocked into action, Lillian's shaky legs propelled her down a dark alley, where she collapsed into a shivering heap. That awful man had actually kicked her! How could anyone be so cruel? How could she be a dog? Lillian was lost in these disturbing thoughts when a vicious mongrel lunged toward her, growling and barking as it attacked. Ouch! It bit her leg! Yelping as she hobbled down the sidewalk, Lillian barely managed to escape.

After wandering for what seemed like an eternity, Lillian was aroused by the marvelous aromas of an Italian deli. Tired and extremely hungry, she slipped through the door as a customer left. But when she sniffed at the showcase, her mouth watering, an overly sensitive diner shrieked, "Get that filthy slobbering mutt out of here!"

Tossed into the alley, Lillian sobbed and sobbed until she found herself surprisingly drawn to the scent of leftovers from an overturned garbage can. Ashamed at her loss of good manners and exquisite taste, she fought a losing battle to turn away from the disgusting scraps.

After eating her fill, Lillain felt alone in the damp, cool darkness. She limped down the alley, and a rope cage fell from the sky, imprisoning her! As she struggled in vain, her heart raced and everything went black.

Lillian regained consciousness in a drab concrete cell. All night long thoughtless dogs in surrounding cells kept her awake with their obnoxious barking and pitiful whining.

*B*y the next morning, Lillian's legs were so stiff and sore she could barely move. As her mind raced with worry about her future, she imagined hearing her mother's voice far in the distance. But wait!

Lillian collapsed into the warm arms of her mother, tears of joy and relief streaming down their cheeks.

When she arrived home,
Lillian felt ashamed to face the rest
of her family. To her surprise, however,
they seemed oblivious to her filthy, smelly
condition and welcomed her with open arms.

Lillian was so happy to be home and to feel
everyone's love, she no longer cared that she was
a dog.

*M*ore than anyone else, the Pekinese seemed ecstatic to see her. Rushing across the room, he kissed all over her dirty little face. And for the first time—but not the last—Lillian kissed back.

# Trisha Adelena Howell

Trisha Howell was inspired to write *The Princess and the Pekinese* while wishing that Lillian, her six-pound Yorkie, would accept Addison, the new arrival who had ended her reign as "only dog." For three years the thirteen-pound Pekinese tried unsuccessfully to befriend the hostile Lillian. The two finally achieved an uneasy truce only after Addison learned to avoid the snooty Yorkie, who imagined herself a human being, or at least a Great Dane.

"But then one day," Trisha says, "I noticed Lillian sitting right next to Addison instead of as far away as possible. Later Addison's paw was around Lillian, and she snuggled up to him rather than snarling. After dinner that night, Lillian suddenly dropped dead from an apparent heart attack. No one was more upset than Addison, who refused to eat, drink or even move for days.

"I met with an animal communicator, who revealed not only how dearly Addison had loved Lillian but also the puzzling news that Lillian's death was due, not to her own illness, but to something she wanted to accomplish.

"A few days later, my husband and I left for a month abroad. Lillian would have been staying with my mother Frances, who now wanted to take Addison home to San Diego for company. Otherwise, he would have stayed in Tonasket with the people who had agreed to care for our German Shepherds Hanna and Alex.

"When we returned from Europe, Hanna and Alex were thin and sickly. They were half starved and had been left outside the whole time exposed to wolf and coyote attacks. If Addison had been in this situation, he surely would have died. Instead, he came home from his visit with Frances looking healthy and pampered. It was then I realized the mysterious reason for Lillian's death—she had given her life to save Addison's."

Trisha and her husband Dean live on 3,000 wilderness acres in the Okanogan Highlands near Tonasket, Washington. The household presently includes caretakers Rich and Bernie Wells, German Shepherds Hanna and Alex, Bailey the Peek-a-Poo, Speedy the Shepherd/Black Lab/Wolf, Shelby the Husky/Shepherd, and Addison (author of *The Pekinese Who Saved Civilization*). Addison can be reached at www.addisonthedog.com. An avid reader and writer, Trisha also enjoys hiking, yoga, golf, travel, movies, playing games and the piano. She can be reached at: trisha@howellcanyonpress.com.

# Paul Lopez

Paul Lopez has loved art since he was a child. A native Californian, he has been illustrating books and posters since 1987. Paul draws inspiration from spending time in the mountains. He is devoted to conserving the environment and has a special affection for mammals and marine life. The illustrator of four books for Howell Canyon Press, he can be reached at: Paul J. Lopez Illustration, 2857 Rhoades Road, San Diego, CA 92139, (619) 479-1426.

# Howell Canyon Press

features health-promoting and uplifting books, videos and CD-ROMS

## THE ADVENTURES OF MELON AND TURNIP
By Trisha Adelena Howell 32 pages hc 8.5" x 11" isbn 1-931210-04-7 $15.95

Come celebrate the joy and wonder of life as best friends Melon and Turnip experience a world of adventure and discovery.

## THE TOWER: AN ADVENTURE
By Trisha Adelena Howell 64 pages sc isbn 1-931210-05-5 $11.95

Twelve-year-old Talia discovers that the old tower near her family's new home is a portal to ancient worlds and other dimensions of reality. She and her friends Daniel and Michelle embark on a series of pulse-racing missions to save the world.

## THE JOURNEYING WORKBOOK:
## HOW TO ADVENTURE TO UNLEASH YOUR INNER POWER
By Trisha Adelena Howell 128 pages sc 8.5" x 11" isbn 1-931210-06-3 $12.95

Shamanic journeying—an avenue to the wisdom of the universe through the depths of your being— is simple and safe for everyone. This practical manual guides you through a series of empowering journeys.

## LIVING IN A GLOWING WORLD
By Trisha Adelena Howell 80 pages sc with b/w photos isbn 1-931210-08-X $9.95

This collection of original poetry celebrates the miracle of life through the six seasons of Winter, Thaw, Spring, Summer, Harvest and Autumn.

## THE PEKINESE WHO SAVED CIVILIZATION
By Sir Addison Silber Howell, Esquire, as told to Trisha Adelena Howell
128 pages sc with b/w photos isbn 1-931210-07-1 $9.95

You've heard that behind every great man is a great woman, but did you know that behind every great human being is a great dog? Addison the Pekinese reveals the true history of the world from the canine perspective. He shows how to solve all global problems, thereby saving civilization.

## NCR: UNLEASH YOUR STRUCTURAL POWER, 3RD EDITION (2001)
By Dean Howell, ND 108 pages sc with b/w photos isbn 1-931210-02-0 $11.95

Testimonials, articles and other vital information about NeuroCranial Restructuring (NCR).

## NCR: THE ULTIMATE CRANIAL THERAPY (2001 VIDEO)
Produced by New Vision Media $24.95

This 110-minute video features a demonstration treatment, testimonials from 16 patients, and explanations about how NCR treatment works.

## NCR: THE ULTIMATE CRANIAL THERAPY (2001 CD-ROM)
Produced by New Vision Media $24.95

A CD-Rom featuring instant navigation to each section of the book and of the 2001 video.

## NCR: THE VIDEO (1996)
Produced by Dean Howell, ND $9.95

This original explanation of NCR remains popular because of its low price and its in-depth presentation of the basic concepts of NeuroCranial Restructuring.

Order online at www.howellcanyonpress.com or write to
Howell Canyon Press, P.O. Box 448, Tonasket, WA 98855 or call (888)252-0411.